자꾸 생각나고
보고 싶고 그래

자꾸 생각나고
보고 싶고 그래

글·그림·애니메이션 퍼엉

arte

책 사용법
How to read

예쁜 그림을 보면서 내용을 상상해보세요.

Imagine the stories inside the beautiful pictures.

QR코드를 찍은 뒤 책 위에 휴대폰을 올려놓고
애니메이션을 봐요.

Scan the QR code and put the cell phone on the book
to watch the animation version.

미공개 애니메이션을 볼 수 있는
특별한 페이지도 있어요!

There are special pages for animations
first shown only through this book!

차례
Contents

우리 처음 만난 날, 기억나요?
The day first we met. Do you remember?

그 사람 얼굴이 머릿속에서 떠나질 않아요.
I can't stop thinking about him.

그녀가 집었던 책을 꺼내 봐요.

I read the book that you picked.

Love is meterial that
anyone can relate to an

I feel that love is some

at emits light from

small things in daily li

and translate them

Tllustrations and anim

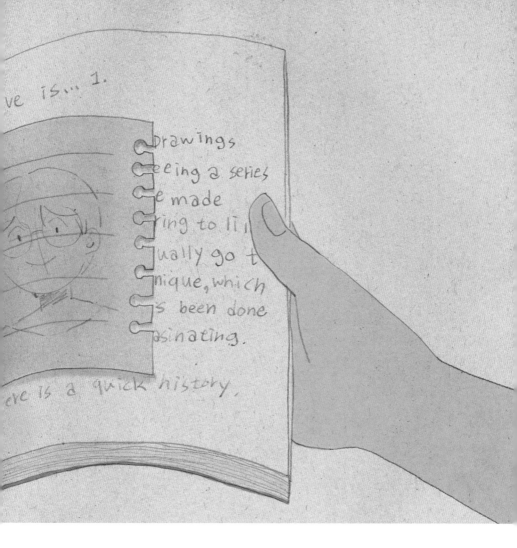

책 속에서 예상치 못한 선물을 발견했어요.
I found an unexpected present inside the book.

오래전 도서관에서
(Long time ago at the library) 2/3

우연히 지나가는 그녀를 봤어요.
I saw you passing by.

두근두근, 조심스럽게 그녀를 향해 다가가요.

I approached you carefully with a beating heart.

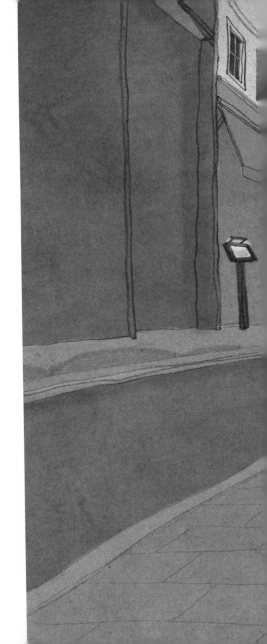

다시 만나게 될 거라고 생각했어요.
I knew we'll meet again.

오래전 도서관에서
(Long time ago at the library) 3/3

Episode 2

첫 데이트
The first date

무슨 옷을 입을까?
What should I wear?

곧 그 사람을 만날 생각에 너무 행복해요!
I'm so happy to meet him soon!

그 사람이 보여요. 이 순간을 오래 기다렸어요.
I see you. I have dreamed of this moment for a long time.

첫 데이트
(The first date) 1/3

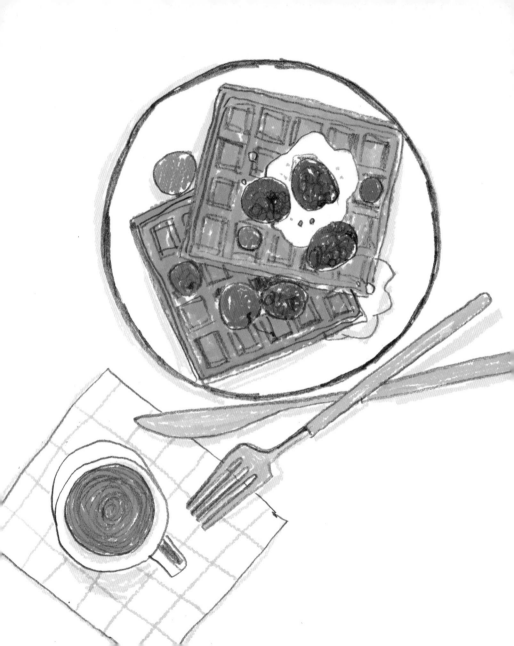

함께 걸어요.
We walked together.

소나기를 만났어요.
Suddenly it rained.

마음에 드는 카페를 발견했어요.
We found a nice café.

첫 데이트
(The first date) 2/3

도서관 앞에서 도시락을 먹었어요.
In front of the library, we had lunch.

정말 맛있었어요. 고마워요.
It was so good. Thank you.

BONUS TRACK

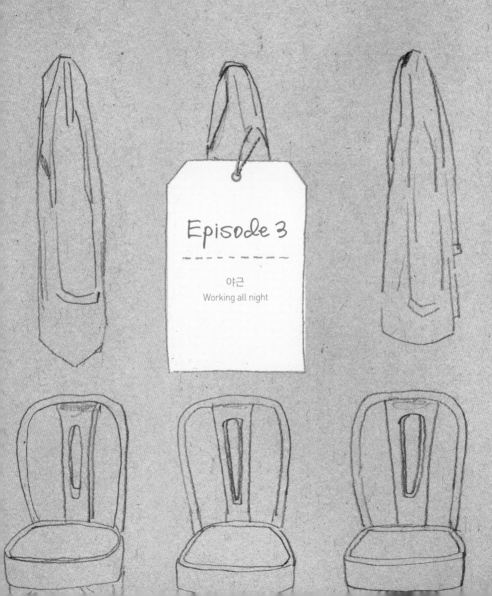

Episode 3

야근
Working all night

일 끝나고 우리 만날까요?
Shall we meet after work?

오늘은 야근을 해야 해요. 그래도 목소리를 들으니 힘이 나요.
I have to work all night. Still, I feel better hearing your voice.

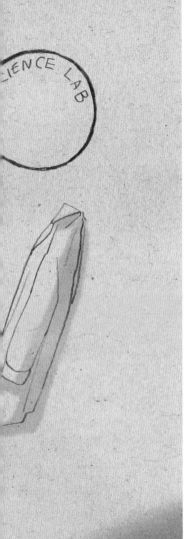

힘들죠? 간식을 사왔어요.

Is everything okay? I bought some snacks for you.

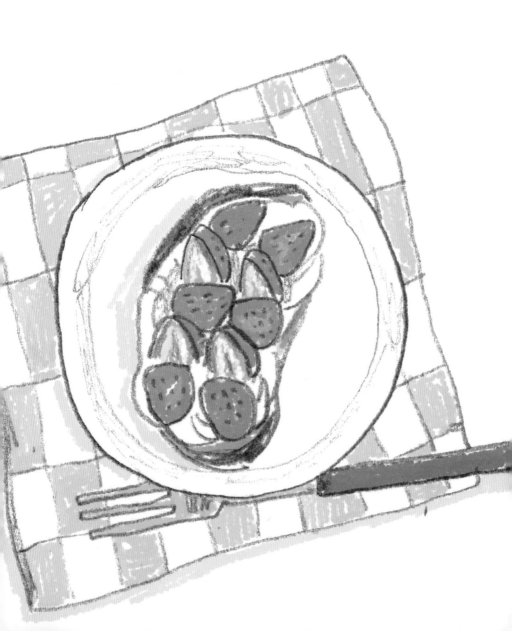

야근
(Working all night) 1/2

헤어지기 아쉬워요.
I don't want to go home.

놀이동산에 놀러 왔어요.
We went to an amusement park.

회전목마를 타요.
We rode a merry-go-round.

야근
(Working all night) 2/2

위 뜨

SWEET

BONUS TRACK

휴대전화로 QR코드를 찍은 뒤
스크린에 올려놓고 감상하세요.
Put your mobile on the screen and enjoy.

어떤 음악을 좋아해요?
What kind of music do you like?

이 노래를 들려주고 싶었어요.

I wanted you to listen to this song.

서로가 추천한 앨범을 샀어요.

We bought music albums we recommended to each other.

꾸벅꾸벅 졸다 그 사람에게 기대요.

I drowsed off and leaned slightly on his shoulder.

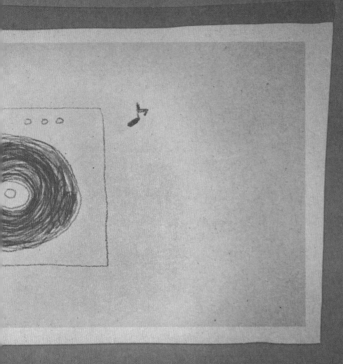

상영 중

BONUS TRACK

휴대전화로 QR코드를 찍은 뒤
스크린에 올려놓고 감상하세요.
Put your mobile on the screen and enjoy.

Episode 5

파티
The party with friends

활짝 웃으며 다가와요.

She walked toward me with a big smile.

친구들과 파티를 했어요.
A party with friends.

친구들 이야기에 푹 빠져들어요.
I'm deeply fell into their stories.

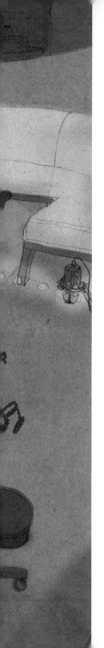

함께 '머스트 댄스'를 해요.

We played a game called 'Must Dance'.

네 친구들은 참 좋은 사람들 같아.
I like your friends.

파티
(The party with friends)

BONUS TRACK

휴대전화로 QR코드를 찍은 뒤
스크린에 올려놓고 감상하세요.
Put your mobile on the screen and enjoy.

Episode 6

바쁜 날
A busy day

오늘은 너에게 연락할 틈도 없이 일했어.
I worked so hard that I couldn't even call you.

바쁘다, 바빠.
So busy!

PUUUNG

와줘서 고마워. 보고 싶었어.

Thanks for coming. I really missed you.

퇴근 후 너와 함께 보내는 시간이 가장 좋아.
I love this time of the day, being with you after work.

바쁜 날
(A busy day)

BONUS TRACK

휴대전화로 QR코드를 찍은 뒤
스크린에 올려놓고 감상하세요.
Put your mobile on the screen and enjoy.

Episode 7

벚꽃
At the lake with
cherry blossom

피크닉 준비를 해요.
I prepared to go picnic.

자전거를 타고 벚꽃 길을 달렸어요.
We rode bicycles on the road full of cherry blossoms.

돗자리 위에 앉아 벚꽃을 구경해요.
We sat on the mat and watched the cherry blossoms.

PUUNG©

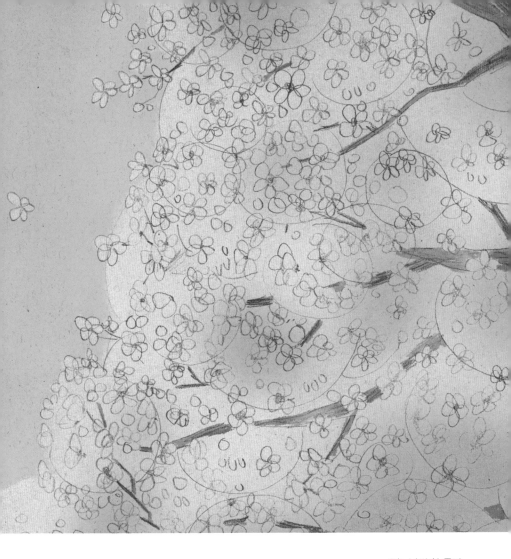

오늘 날씨 참 좋다.
Nice weather today.

BONUS TRACK

휴대전화로 QR코드를 찍은 뒤
스크린에 올려놓고 감상하세요.
Put your mobile on the screen and enjoy.

Episode 8

키스
Kiss

첫 키스
A frist kiss

두근두근, 설레서 잠이 오질 않아요.
I can't fall asleep because of you.

친구에게 남자 친구를 소개했어요.
I introduced my boyfriend to my friend.

손을 잡고 걸어요.
We walked hand in hand.

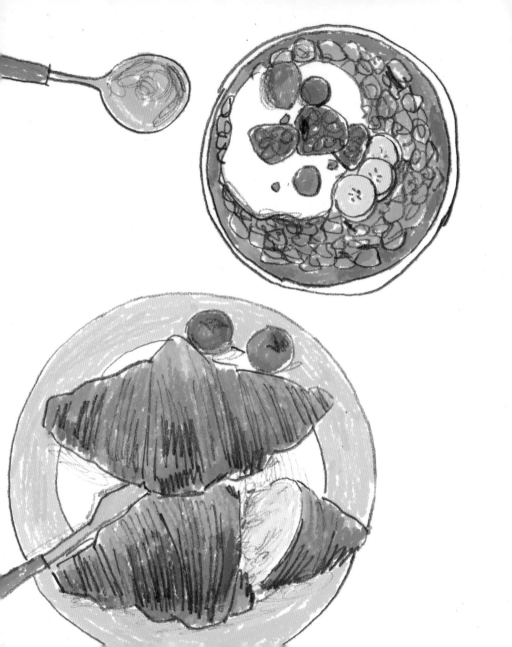

BONUS TRACK

휴대전화로 QR코드를 찍은 뒤
스크린에 올려놓고 감상하세요.
Put your mobile on the screen and enjoy.

Episode 9

고양이 가필드
The cat, Garfield

쓰러진 길고양이를 만났어요.

I found a cat lying on the road.

함께 고양이에 대해 공부해요.
We studied about cats.

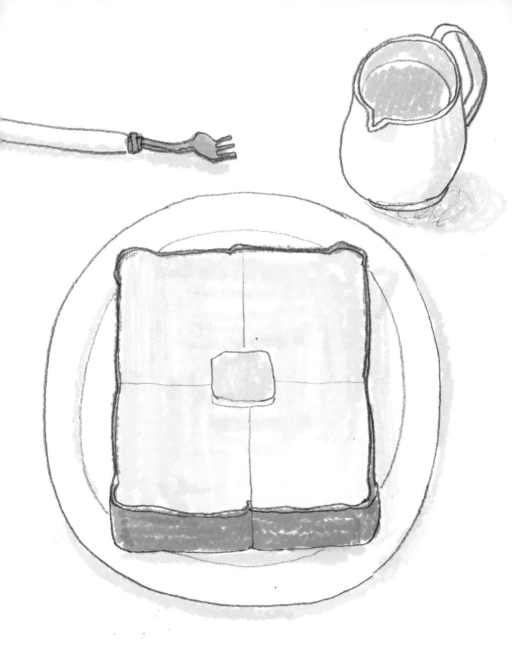

가필드에게 캣타워를 선물해줬어요. 쓰담쓰담.
I gave a cat tower to Garfield.

우리 잘 지내보자, 가필드!
Let's get closer. Garfield!

한가한 주말 아침, 밖으로 나왔어요.
I went out in the morning of a free weekend.

누구게?
Guess who?

커피를 마시며 한적한 거리를 바라봐요.

We looked at the quiet street while drinking coffee.

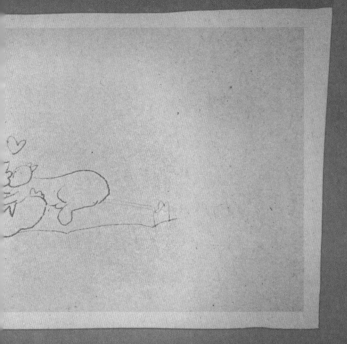

BONUS TRACK

Episode 10

별을 봐요

Stargazing

별을 보러 가요. 어두컴컴한 숲속을 달려요.
We went to see the stars. We passed through the dark forest.

와, 별이 쏟아질 것 같아!
There are so many stars!

여러 별들을 관측했어요.
We looked at the stars.

별을 봐요
(Stargazing)

BONUS TRACK

휴대전화로 QR코드를 찍은 뒤
스크린에 올려놓고 감상하세요.
Put your mobile on the screen and enjoy

Episode 11

- - - - - - - - - - -

남자 친구 집에 놀러 갔어요

I went to over his place

내가 맛있는 요리해줄게!
I'll cook delicious food.

고마워요! 잘 먹겠습니다!

Thanks for the lovely meal.

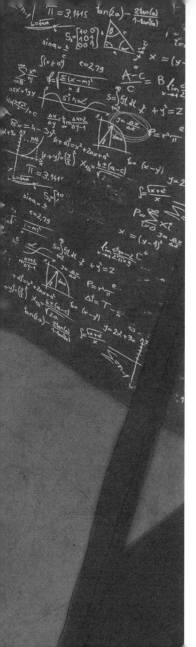

어린 시절 앨범을 구경해요.

We saw pictures of his childhood in an old album.

저는 해가 떠오르기 직전의 새벽이 좋아요.

I like the dawn just before the sun rises.

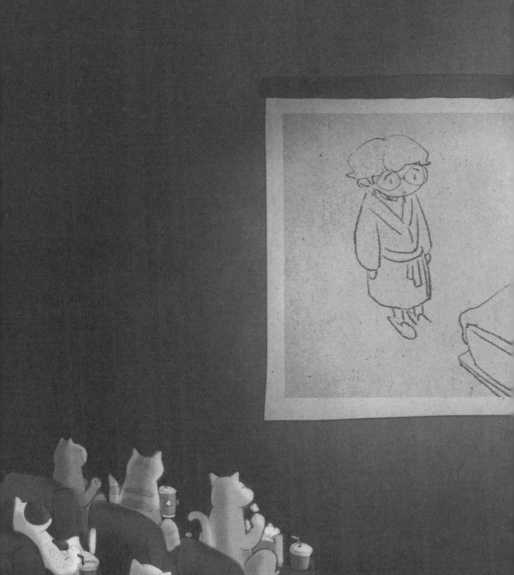

BONUS TRACK

휴대전화로 QR코드를 찍은 뒤
스크린에 올려놓고 감상하세요.
Put your mobile on the screen and enjoy.

Episode 12

함께 조깅을 해요
Jogging together

함께 조깅을 해요.
We went jogging together.

LOVE IS

함께 조깅을 해요
(Jogging together)

BONUS TRACK

휴대전화로 QR코드를 찍은 뒤
스크린에 올려놓고 감상하세요.
Put your mobile on the screen and enjoy.

Episode 13

함께 추억을 만들어요
Making memories with you

하루 종일 비가 내려요.
It rained all day.

도서관에서 여행지 책을 봤어요.

We read a book about travel destinations in the library.

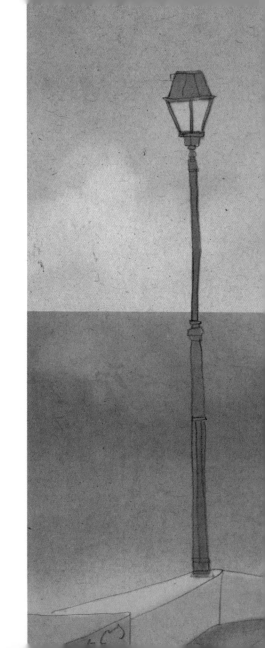

바다에 놀러 왔어요.
We went to the beach.

계단에 앉아서 바다에 대한 추억들을 이야기해요.

We sat on the stairs and talked about our memories in the beach.

시원한 파도 소리를 들으며 아이스크림을 먹어요.
We ate icecream listening to the sound of waves.

철썩이는 파도를 멍하니 바라봐요.
We stared at the splashing waves.

함께 추억을 만들어요
(Making memories with you) 2/3

바닷마을에서 열린 플리마켓을 구경해요.
We looked around a flea market near the beach.

예쁜 커플 팔찌를 샀어요.

We bought fancy bracelets for a couple.

함께 추억을 만들어요
(Making memories with you) 3/3

BONUS TRACK

휴대전화로 QR코드를 찍은 뒤
스크린에 올려놓고 감상하세요.
Put your mobile on the screen and enjoy.

Episode 14

소개팅
A blind date

친구를 도와 함께 카페 알바를 했어요.
We worked part-time at a café for my friend.

COFFEE 2.5
ESPRESO 3.0
LATTE 3.0
CHOCO 3.0

어색하지만 잘해보고 싶어요.

It's awkward, but I really want to have a good time with her.

날씨도 좋고, 커피 향도 좋고, 음악도 좋고, 분명히 잘될 거예요.

Everything will be fine because the weather is nice, coffee smells good, and the music is great.

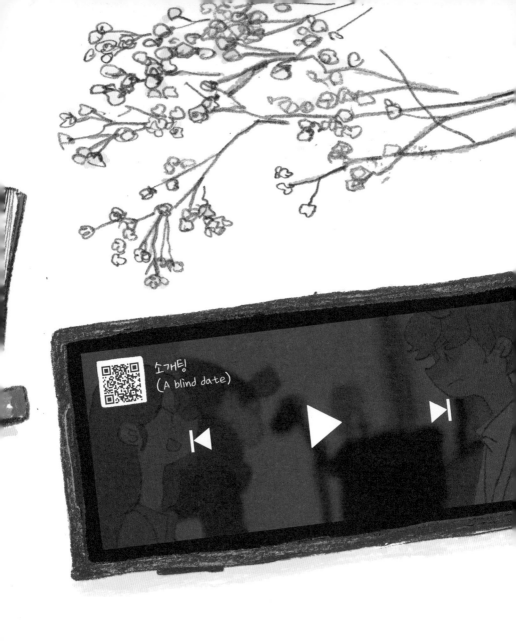

소개팅
(A blind date)

BONUS TRACK

휴대전화로 QR코드를 찍은 뒤
스크린에 올려놓고 감상하세요.
Put your mobile on the screen and enjoy.

Episode 15

네가 내 꿈에 나왔어
You appeared in my dream

야근을 하다가 잠깐 눈을 붙여요.

I slept for a few minutes while working at night.

꿈에 네가 나왔어요.
You appeared in my dream.

너는 꿈속에서도 멋지네.

You are amazing in the dream, too.

네가 내 꿈에 나왔어
(You appeared in my dream)

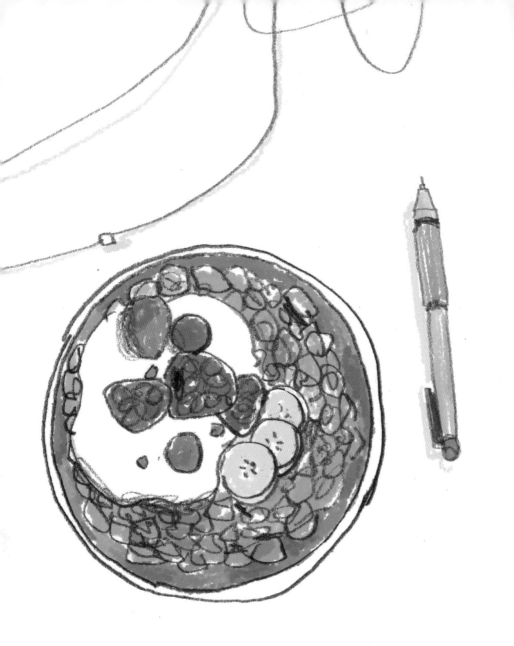

BONUS TRACK

휴대전화로 QR코드를 찍은 뒤
스크린에 올려놓고 감상하세요.
Put your mobile on the screen and enjoy.

Episode 16

커퍼런스
An academic conference

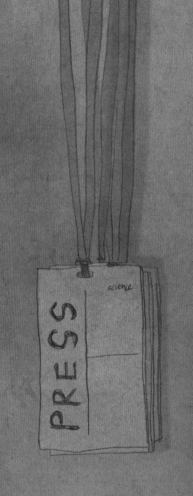

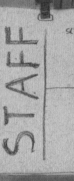

과학 컨퍼런스에 왔어요.

I went to a science conference.

네가 일하는 모습은 정말 멋있어!
You look great while working.

컨퍼런스
(An academic conference)

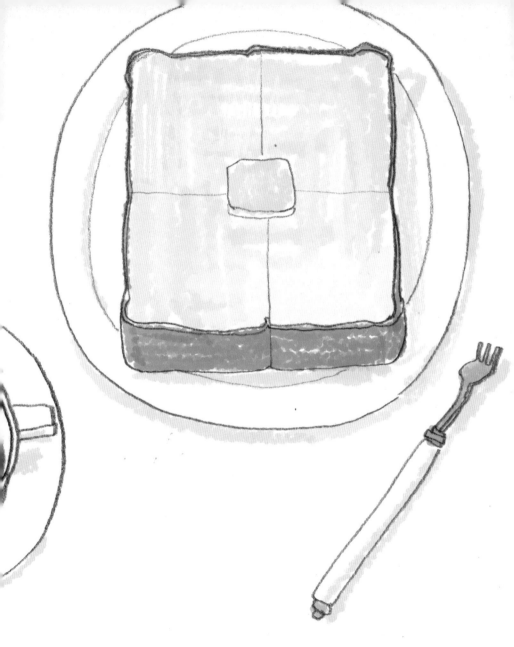

BONUS TRACK

휴대전화로 QR코드를 찍은 뒤
스크린에 올려놓고 감상하세요.
Put your mobile on the screen and enjoy.

Episode 17

휴가
A vacation

푸르른 시골로 휴가를 왔어요.

We went to the countryside for a vacation.

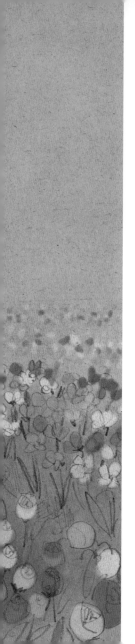

꽃보다 네가 더 예뻐.
You are more beautiful than flowers.

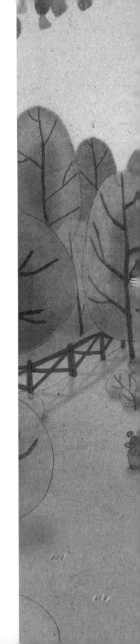

멋진 숙소의 강아지가 우릴 반겨요.
A dog welcomed us.

무서운 이야기를 해요. 등골이 오싹해요!
We shared scary stories. Spooky!

지저귀는 새소리에 아침 일찍 잠에서 깼어요.
I woke up early in the morning because of the birds singing.

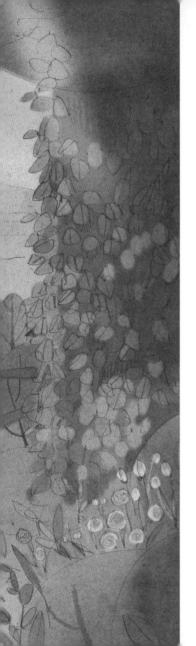

시원한 나무 그늘 아래에서 커피를 마셔요.
We enjoyed coffee under the tree.

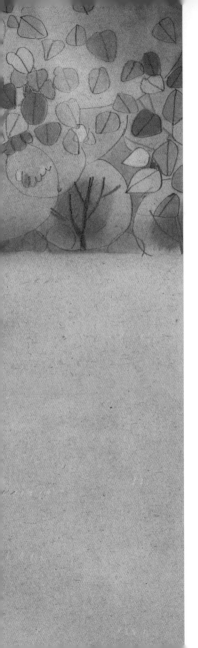

그네를 밀어줬어요. 더 높이높이!

He pushed the swing for me. Higher!

소파 위 이불 속에 쏙 들어가 잠깐 잠들었어요.
We took a nap inside the cosy blanket on the sofa.

풀벌레 소리를 들으며 저녁을 먹어요.
We had dinner enjoying a gentle rustle in the grass.

휴가
(A vacation) 2/2

상영 중

BONUS TRACK

휴대전화로 QR코드를 찍은 뒤
스크린에 올려놓고 감상하세요.
Put your mobile on the screen and enjoy.

Episode 18

안녕
Goodbye

소파를 사러 왔어요. 엄청 푹신푹신해!

We went to buy a sofa. It's so comfortable!

소파에 앉아 이야기를 해요.
We talked together on the sofa.

장기 출장을 떠나기 전날, 집에서 맛있는 간식을 먹으며 놀았어요.

We spent time together mostly eating snacks and talking the day before she left for her business trip.

안녕
(Goodbye) 2/3

잘 다녀와요.
Goodbye. Take care.

네가 탄 비행기일까? 떠오르는 비행기가 시야에서 사라질 때까지 한참을 바라봤어요.

Would that be the one you're on? I stared at the plane until it finally disappeared out of my sight.

너와의 추억으로 가득찬 이 도시가 보이지 않을 때까지, 한참을 바라봤어요.
I looked down at the city full of memories with you until it completely faded away.

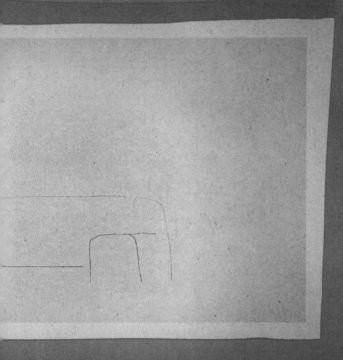

BONUS TRACK

휴대전화로 QR코드를 찍은 뒤
스크린에 올려놓고 감상하세요.
Put your mobile on the screen and enjoy.

KI신서 8780

자꾸 생각나고 보고 싶고 그래

1판 1쇄 인쇄 2019년 11월 30일
1판 1쇄 발행 2019년 12월 6일

지은이 퍼엉
펴낸이 김영곤
펴낸곳 (주)북이십일 21세기북스

콘텐츠개발3팀장 최유진
책임편집 위윤녕 **디자인** urbook

마케팅팀 배상현 김보희 박화인 한경화
출판영업팀 한충희 오서영 윤승환
제작팀 이영민 권경민

출판등록 2000년 5월 6일 제406-2003-061호
주소 (10881) 경기도 파주시 회동길 201(문발동)
대표전화 031-955-2100 **팩스** 031-955-2151 **이메일** book21@book21.co.kr

ⓒ 퍼엉, 2019
ISBN 978-89-509-8436-6 03810

(주)북이십일 경계를 허무는 콘텐츠 리더

21세기북스 채널에서 도서 정보와 다양한 영상자료, 이벤트를 만나세요!
페이스북 facebook.com/jiinpill21 **포스트** post.naver.com/21c_editors
인스타그램 instagram.com/jiinpill21 **홈페이지** www.book21.com
유튜브 www.youtube.com/book21pub

서울대 가지 않아도 들을 수 있는 명강의! 〈서가명강〉
유튜브, 네이버, 팟빵, 팟캐스트에서 '서가명강'을 검색해보세요!